Tumbleweed Baby

By Anna Myers

Illustrated by Charles Vess

ABRAMS BOOKS FOR YOUNG READERS

New York

The art in this book was drawn on Strathmore Series 500 Bristol using FW colored inks and Prismacolor colored pencils.

Library of Congress Cataloging-in-Publication Data

Myers, Anna.
    Tumbleweed Baby / by Anna Myers ; illustrations, Charles Vess.
        pages cm
    Summary: Long ago in Nowhere, Texas, Mama and Papa Upagainstit agree to take in the wild baby their five children find in a passing tumbleweed, despite the objections of the one who used to be "the littlest-of-all girl."
        ISBN 978-1-4197-1232-6
    [1. Family life—Texas—Fiction. 2. Foundlings—Fiction. 3. Feral children—Fiction. 4. Texas—Fiction. 5. Tall tales.] I. Vess, Charles, illustrator. II. Title.
    PZ7.M9814Tv 2014
    [Fic]—dc23
    2013042640

Text copyright © 2014 Anna Myers
Illustrations copyright © 2014 Charles Vess

Book design by Chad W. Beckerman

Published in 2014 by Abrams Books for Young Readers, an imprint of ABRAMS. All rights reserved. No portion of this book may be reproduced, stored in a retrieval system, or transmitted in any form or by any means, mechanical, electronic, photocopying, recording, or otherwise, without written permission from the publisher.

Printed and bound in China

10 9 8 7 6 5 4 3 2 1

Abrams Books for Young Readers are available at special discounts when purchased in quantity for premiums and promotions as well as fundraising or educational use. Special editions can also be created to specification. For details, contact specialsales@abramsbooks.com or the address below.

ABRAMS
THE ART OF BOOKS SINCE 1949

115 West 18th Street
New York, NY 10011
www.abramsbooks.com

To our two babies, Isaac Matthew
Myers and Cecilia Louise Lane,
who were not found in tumbleweeds.
—A.M.

To everyone who has plucked their
very own "baby" out of the thicket
of their imagination and used
it to change the world.
—C.V.

A long time ago, at the edge of Nowhere, Texas, was a falling-apart house, all filled up with the Upagainstit family. Mama and Papa Upagainstit had five children: a biggish boy, a medium boy, a smallest boy, a not-so-big girl, and a littlest-of-all girl. All around the falling-apart house there was nothing but sand and—oh yes—tumbleweeds, tumbleweeds everywhere.

One day when the Upagainstit children were walking home from school, the biggish boy got knocked right over by a tumbleweed. "Looky there at that," said the smallest boy, and he pointed straight at a foot sticking out, plain as day, from the tumbleweed.

"Stand back," said the biggish boy, and he got up off the ground. "I'd better see what's inside that weed."

And so he found her! Right in the middle of that tumbleweed he found a baby, and he pulled that Tumbleweed Baby out.

"She's a wild-all-over baby," said the littlest-of-all girl. "Put her back."

"I like her smile," said the medium boy.

"I like her hair," said the smallest boy.

"I like her toes," said the not-so-big girl.

"I just plain like her," said the biggish boy. "Let's take her home."

So they did.

They set her on the floor of the falling-apart house. "What should we do with this Tumbleweed Baby?" said Papa Upagainstit.

"She's a wild-all-over baby," said the littlest-of-all girl. "We can't keep her."

"Hmm," said Mama. "We'll have to study on that. But right now, we got to give this baby a bath."

The biggish boy went out to draw water.
The medium boy fetched the tin tub, and
Mama got the soap.

The Tumbleweed Baby did not care for baths.
"She is sure enough wild," said Mama.

Supper came next. The Tumbleweed Baby *did* care for supper. She cared for it way too much.

Mama looked at Papa, and they both shook their heads.

"Give her another chance," said the smallest boy.

"We can quiet her down," said the medium boy.

The medium boy picked her up, and
the Upagainstit family gathered around
the baby. They sang a song to her about
tumbling tumbleweeds, all except the
littlest-of-all girl, who didn't.

When they were finished, they set her down on the couch, but she did not stay. "I'll read to her," said the not-so-big girl, and she got out her book about Dick and Jane.

The Tumbleweed Baby did not care for stories.

"Maybe she's riled from needing sleep," said Papa. "Let's turn in."

Mama tucked her in between the two girls, but the Tumbleweed Baby did not care for bed.

All night there was a terrible ruckus in
the falling-apart house.

"We got to talk about this baby," said Papa. "Don't see as we can keep her."

"Soon as it's light," said Mama, and her voice was sad. All the Upagainstit children felt sad, too, except the littlest-of-all girl, who didn't.

At daylight, they gathered around the table for the meeting. The biggish boy held the Tumbleweed Baby tight. "All right," said Papa, "say your piece."

"She's a wild-all-over baby," said the littlest-of-all girl. "We can't keep her."

"But holding her will make me strong for arm wrestling," said the biggish boy.

"She likes my singing," said the medium boy. "I can practice on her for when I get to be a radio singer."

"Chasing after her will make me faster for recess races," said the smallest boy.

"Getting her to like stories will be good practice for being a teacher when I grow up," said the not-so-big girl.

Everyone looked at Mama. "When I give her baths, if you all grabbed a rag, the floors could be mopped in a flash."

Everyone looked at Papa. "I don't know," he said.
Just then the Tumbleweed Baby leaned over to kiss Papa's
cheek. "We got to keep her," Papa said.

Everybody cheered, all except the littlest-of-all girl, who didn't.
After breakfast, Mama held the Tumbleweed Baby tight while
they talked about a name for her.

Papa liked Betty. Mama favored Joan. All three of the boys wanted to name the baby Linda.

"Name her Sauerkraut," said the littlest-of-all girl, who did not
like sauerkraut, not even one little bit.

"Let's let her choose, when she is bigger," said the not-so-big
girl.

So the Upagainstit family did not name their new child, but
they loved her, loved almost all the wildness right out of her.
They called her Tumbleweed Baby, and when she felt too
old to be called Baby, she chose a name for herself.

She named herself Betty Joan Linda Sauerkraut Upagainstit.

And on that day, the day of the naming, the girl who used to be the littlest-of-all girl whispered in Betty Joan Linda Sauerkraut's ear.

"I have a secret to tell you, sister," she said. "I was a Tumbleweed Baby, too."

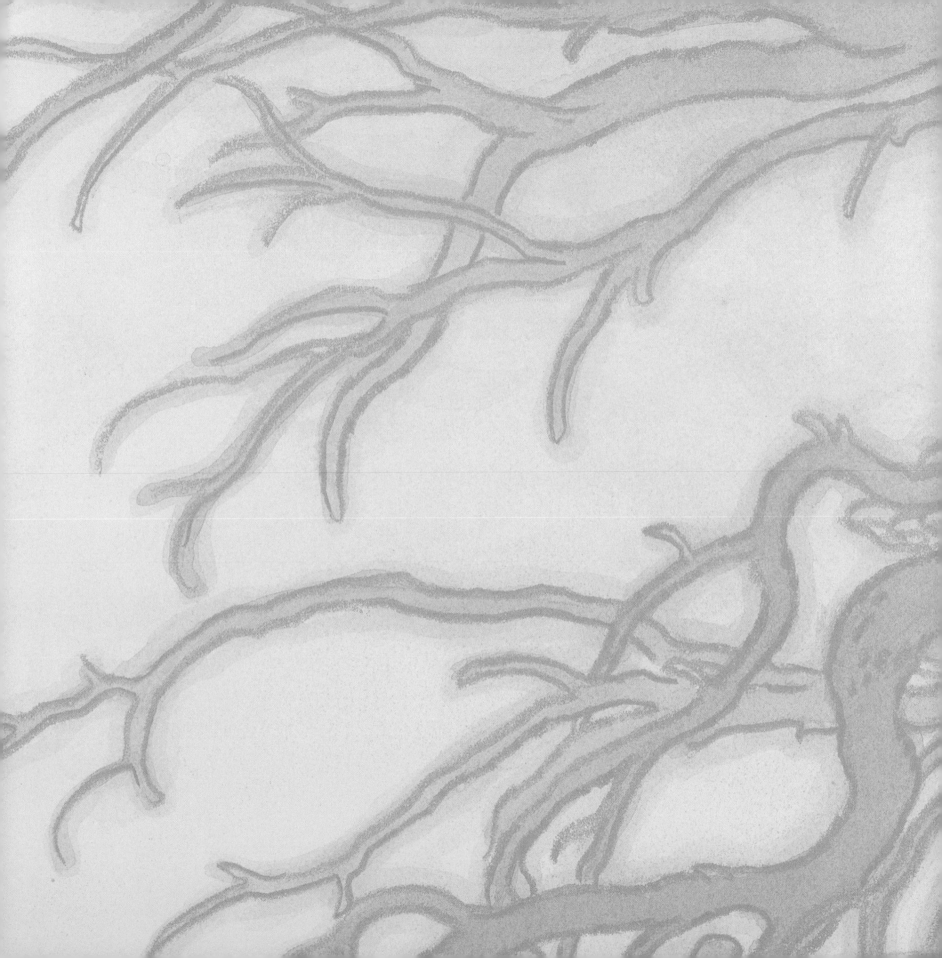